D0563587

Lena Carls

and the

Power of Friendship

ENIOLUWANIMI SOLARU

DEDICATION

To my dad for making this book possible!

Table of Contents

Introduction

Hey there! My name is Lena. Lena Carls! I have to share this with you: Something amazing happened to me last week. I moved to Norco, California, and now I have some awesome, new friends.

You might be wondering why I moved. Well, I moved so that I could get my own room! You might be thinking that is weird, so, to be honest, I'm not sure why we moved, but we did! And now, we live closer to Grandma, Aunt Sophie, Uncle John, and cousin Keila.

We lived in New York City, but even though I miss my old friends, living here is so much fun.

"Lena!"

Oops! Time to go! My mom's calling...

Enjoy!

Chapter 1

Moving

"Stop!" my sister Lilly said.

Why was she saying 'stop'? I was just about to answer that: because I was tickling her. Right now, we are on a train. A very slow one.

"Okay, that is enough, Lena," said Dad.

"Okay, okay, okay!" I said, giggling.

"Here we are!" Dad said when we got there. It was obvious he would say that when we got there.

Because, when else would he say it?

I got up from my cozy seat to follow my family.

"Welcome to Horse Town, USA," said a sign outside the window.

"Yup!" said Mom getting up.

"Come on," urged Dad, walking towards the doors.

"Watch your step on your way out!" said a skinny man with a tall hat.

"Thanks!" I said and gave him a fake smile as I stepped on the ground.

"Don't you love that...fresh air?" said Dad sniffing the air in disgust.

"All I smell is manure," I said. Manure is another word for horse poop. It just sounds less inappropriate, so I started saying manure instead.

"Oh, Lena!" Mom said, rolling her eyes.

"No, really!" I said.

"Okay, that's enough," said Dad. Mom picked Lilly up, which I think is weird because Lilly is **five** years old.

We went to the train station and got an Uber. It's pretty much a taxi, but they don't have taxis here.

"Wow!" said Mom as we arrived at our new home. "That is big." Actually, it was bigger than it looked online!

"Yup!" Dad said. "Keila lives about 10 minutes away." Keila is our cousin.

"That's awesome!" I said. "Also, we need more furniture."

"I think that will change our budget," Mom said. Budget is just another word for money plan. "But we do have some furniture from the attic in our old house."

"Okay," I said as I walked closer to the door. I almost forgot to breathe as I walked into the entrance. There sat the biggest, grandest, most golden chandelier of all time. Lilly stopped walking because she was so surprised about such a giant chandelier, so Mom carried her. At the same time, my dad explained we were in the dining room.

Next, we went to the kitchen, living room, balcony, and more. Then, finally, my bedroom. "Wow!" I said. It was the size of a princess bedroom. The best part was, it was all mine. No sharing this time!

"Get settled in," Mom said.

"Great!" I said back. I had six boxes, so there was not much to do. In half an hour, I was done and went downstairs for dinner.

When I got there, my mom was waiting impatiently.

"What took you so long?" she asked me.

"I got lost," I said as I sat across from Mom, next to Lilly. Dad sat next to Mom. We had mashed potatoes and spinach. Lilly said she was getting sick because of the spinach, but I didn't believe her. Mom didn't believe her either, so she did not get any chocolate cookies. When we were done, I went upstairs. I also got lost again! I mean, who can blame me? This house is gigantic! When I got to my room, I caught my parents putting down my bed. They beat me to my room!

Chapter 2
Let Us be Friends

I woke up to the sound of my purple alarm ringing. I really like that it has a ballet dancer that sings. I went to the bathroom, used the toilet, brushed my teeth, and took a bath. I put on a purple top with strawberries on it. Then I brushed my hair and went downstairs for breakfast. I obviously got lost again. Then, I met my family at the breakfast table. Lilly and I both ate tiger cereal. My parents had, of course, coffee. Just the usual grown-up stuff. Practical adults! They can be so boring sometimes!

"Time to go!" I said, getting up. I walked to the doorway.

"Me too!" Lilly said. She can be annoying sometimes and always wants to do what I do!

Overall, she is my sister, and I do not know what I would do without her.

Dad got our backpacks. Mine is the pink one, with purple and blue polka dots. Lilly's is white with a golden retriever on it.

"Here you go!" Dad said, closing his eyes while giving us our backpacks. Guess what? He gave us the wrong ones! I had Lilly's backpack, and Lilly had mine!

"You are funny!" Lilly said, laughing. I took my backpack from Lilly. Lilly took hers from me. We walked out the door and hopped into the car.

"Are you ready to go?" Mom asked us as she put the keys into the keyhole.

"Vroom, vroom!" Lilly said as she moved her arms and legs everywhere. I giggled.

"Beep, beep!" I said.

"Agent Mom departing from the space station!"

"3...2...1... Blast off!" we all said. And the car started moving. First, Mom dropped Lilly off at Norco Elementary School.

"Bye!" I said.

"Yeah, yeah, see you!" Lilly said.

"Okay, bye!" Mom said. Then, Lilly shut the car door and walked to the entrance. We drove two minutes more, and then I saw a building that said Norco Intermediate School. "This is it!" Mom said.

"Okay, so, see you later, I guess?" I said.

"Bye!" Mom said. I got out of the car and closed the door.

"Here I go!" I said to myself. I walked towards the entrance.

When I got to the entrance, I took a deep breath and walked in.

I looked around and saw a woman.

"Hello!" She said. "You must be Lena Carls!"

"I am, and who are you?" I asked.

"Mrs. Crater, the principal. Your class is right down the hall. Your first class is science. The teacher is Mrs. Salmon," she said. "You missed morning announcements, but you don't really need to hear them. Oh! Take this, fill it out and return it to me tomorrow morning." She handed me some papers. I looked at the papers. "Electives," the paper said at the top. "We need to know what classes you want to take. Remember you are required to take math, English, history, and science. Return it to me on Monday morning."

"Okay!" I said. Then I slid the papers into my backpack and walked down the hall.

The door said, "Mrs. Salmon's Sensational Scholars." I walked in and saw several students in the class. I sat down at a desk which said, "Lena Carls."

"You must be the new girl Mrs. Salmon has been talking about all week," said a girl sitting next to me.

"I'm Lena!" I said. Then I heard the teacher telling us to unpack.

"Follow me!" the girl said, standing up. She put out her hand. I put out mine, and the next thing I knew, she pulled me up. She took me in the same direction as all the other kids. We went out the door to a room not too far from the entrance. It was a room filled with lockers.

"Wow!" I said in amazement.

"Come on! Your locker is next to mine!" she said. I opened my locker and watched the girl do the same. Then as soon as she opened it, she put her backpack in. I took my backpack off and put it in my locker too. Then, I went back and sat down at my desk.

"Welcome, class!" said a woman with pink, rosy cheeks and a bright, blond bun.

"Good morning, Mrs. Salmon!" shouted the whole class.

"We have a new student!" Mrs. Salmon said. I felt myself blush. "Come on up, Lena!" she said. I forced myself up and dragged my feet along the ground as I walked to the front of the class. All the way to the front, I saw people staring at me.

As soon as I got there, I said "hi," but it was so quiet, the front row could hardly hear anything.

"What?" a boy with a green sweater in the second row asked. "You speak so quietly; I can hear a teacher three classrooms away louder!" I was embarrassed, so I looked down at my shoes.

"Do not say mean things in this class. I told you already," Mrs. Salmon said.

"That was not mean; I was just honest! Is there a rule against being honest in this class now?" the boy asked.

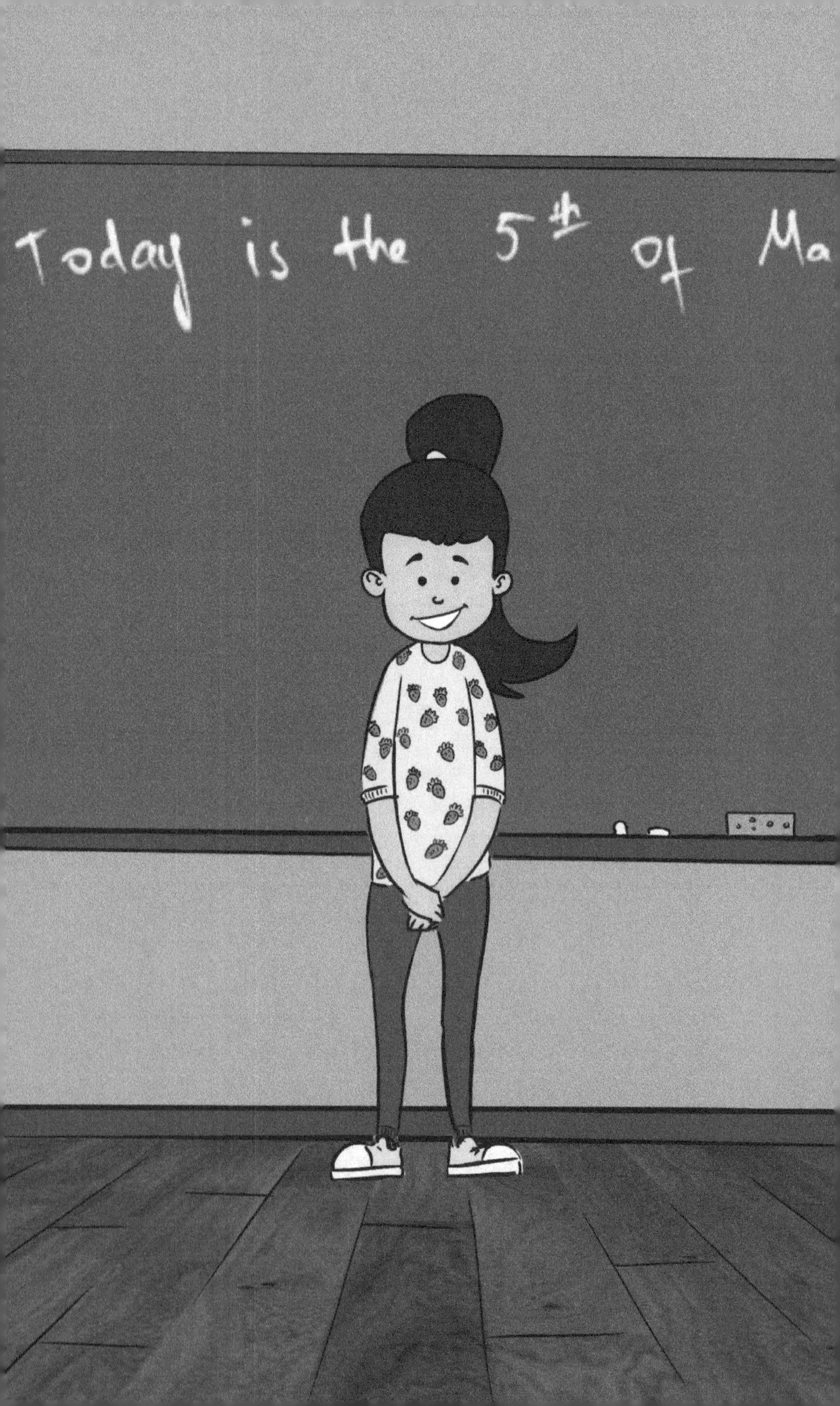
Today is the 5th of Ma

"Michael, either sit quietly in your seat or march yourself down to Mrs. Crater," Mrs. Salmon said. The boy, I mean Michael, pretended to zip his lips. "Lena, you were saying?"

"Hi, everyone!" I said louder this time. The girl who was sitting next to me gave me a thumbs up.

"Okay, now Lena, would you like to choose a student to help you adjust to this change?" Mrs. Salmon asked.

"Yes," I said. That second, everyone's hand shot up. Well, everyone was raising their hand except for Michael. He was turned around on his chair doing criss-cross apple sauce.

"Michael! I've told you that is not safe!" Mrs. Salmon said. Michael turned around and sat properly in his chair.

"You," I said, pointing.

"Go tap their shoulder," Mrs. Salmon said. I walked back to the fourth row and tapped on the girl who sat next to me. She got up.

"Okay, Lucy, show Lena around the school," Mrs. Salmon said.

Lucy pushed open the door, and we walked out just as Mrs. Salmon announced that we would be learning about the code on a computer. We walked down the hall in front of our class.

"Hey Lena, have you seen any horses yet?" Lucy asked me.

"Horses?" I asked. My jaw dropped open. Lucy nodded.

Chapter 3
Hay Is for Horses

"Hey! Hello!" I blinked twice. Lucy was staring right at me.

"Hay is for horses," I said. I smiled and waited for a reply. Lucy laughed.

"I wonder if hay is entirely disgusting," Lucy said.

"Yuck!" I said.

"Let's go to the gym," Lucy said. "It's right over there," Lucy said, pointing to two big, brown doors. "You should meet Mrs. Marten!"

"Okay!" I said. We started moving and pushed open the doors.

"Wow!" I said. The room was a basketball court.

There were different colored baskets with tags to tell which gym items were in which basket.

"Hello!" said a friendly voice.

"Hi!" I replied. "Are you Mrs. Marten?"

"Yes, I am!" she said. "Lucy must have told you, huh?"

"She did!" I said. Mrs. Marten had one of those sweatbands, which are supposed to stop you from sweating, but they mostly make you feel cooler while running. "If you want to make it all the way around the school, or at least halfway before history class, then you need to get going,"

"Okay," I said. I turned to the door. But guess what? Lucy was not there!

"Do you know where Lucy is?" I asked Mrs. Marten. She had her hands on her hips and moved her eyebrows to the left. "Huh?" I asked, and I looked to the left. Lucy was dribbling a basketball.

She was about to make the shot. She shot! she scored!

"GOAL!" We all cheered!

"And the crowd goes wild!" Lucy said.

"Wow! How did you get so good?" I asked.

"Lucy is on the school basketball team," Mrs. Marten said.

"Only the best!" Lucy said, showing her muscles. I raised an eyebrow.

"Go! There are so many more sights to see!" Mrs. Marten said.

"Bye!" I said. Then we walked out the door. We went to five more amazing classrooms and met six more amazing people.

We went to the library and met Miss Jones and Mr. Walkman. We went to the art room and met Mr. Miller. We went to the computer lab and met Mrs. Ally. We went to music class and met Mrs. Clady, and last, we went to math class and met Mr. Melvin.

Soon, we made it back to class and had math, history, art, lunch, and then recess. After that, it was time for the library. I sat in between Mary and Lucy. They began to fight over colors for the poster, subjects for the poster, and, most importantly, me!

"You are already friends with Ruby!" Mary argued to Lucy.

"For the last time! I can have more than one friend, you know!" Lucy argued back. How come they were arguing? It was a long story, so to make a long story short, I helped Mary with soccer at the gym, and now she thinks I am her best friend.

"I'm both of your friends!" I said. Lucy and Mary turned their backs. "Oh, brother!" I said.

***

Later, I was sitting on a bench in the cafeteria. But I was not eating. In fact, no one was. We were all waiting. Why would we be waiting? You could say we were waiting for our numbers to be called, or you could say we were waiting because adults can be a bunch of slowpokes. Either way, we were still waiting.

"23!" I heard from the walkie-talkie.

"23!" Assistant Principal Miss Malory repeated. Michael got up from behind me. Then, he did the most disgusting thing. He burped in my face.

"Michael!" Lucy said. Yes, Lucy was sitting right next to me. She was a car rider too.

"Sorry, didn't mean to!" He said, walking to the exit.

"Everyone out!" said the walkie-talkie.

"Everyone out!" Miss Malory repeated. Lucy held my hand. We both got up and walked to the exit with the others.

"Lena!" I heard when I get outside. That is weird! What is so weird? It was Mom's voice. Just then, I saw Mom's car at the back of the drive-thru pick-up. The window was down.

"Mom!" I said, running to the car. I opened the car door and slid in. "Where is Lilly?" I asked, looking in the back seats. "Oh, her school was over 30 minutes ago, but I was still at work."

"Oh, where do you work?"

"18 minutes away, at the post office, but I'm still taking some exams to become a nurse."

"Okay, let's go pick up Lilly," I said. The car started up, and we started moving. Two minutes later, we were right in front of Norco Elementary School.

"Stay in the car. I'll be right back," Mom told me.

"Okay," I said. Right after she left, my phone vibrates in my back pocket. Lucy texted me! How? I gave her my number during recess.

Hey Lena, I was wondering if you wanted to come to my house to do our homework.

Sure, but I need to ask my mom first.

I answered.

Ask her. If she says yes, I will text you the address.

Lucy replied.

Then Mom came back with Lilly and saw me on my phone. "Who are you texting?" Mom asked as she buckled Lilly up.

"My new friend, Lucy!" I told her.

"A new buddy on the first day! Sweet! So, I can tell you had a good day," Mom said.

"Yeah, pretty good!" I said.

"Well, what did she say?" Mom asked me as she buckled herself in.

"If I could come to her house to do our homework."

"Well, as long as you don't get distracted and only play afterward, okay?" The car started moving.

"Yes!" I said.

"Now Lilly, how was your day?" Mom asked.

"Great!" Lilly said. Lilly started to tell Mom all about her day.

She said yes!

I texted back.

Two minutes later, I got a reply.

Sweet! 1111152 Driftwood

"Eek!" I screeched.

"What's wrong?" Mom asked.

"Nothing, it's just that Lucy lives in our neighborhood!" I said.

"Oh! What a treat!" Mom said, "Let's go home, get your snack and go!"

"Great!" I said.

***

Five minutes later, we made it home. As I got out of the car, I saw Dad's car pull up into the parking lot. He is a math teacher for high school students.

"Dad!" I said, running to him.

"Daddy!" Lilly said, flinging herself into his arms.

"Hello girls," Dad said.

"Dad, I'm going to my friend Lucy's house. Can I get my after-school snack and go?" I asked. I must have said something funny because, next, Dad chuckled.

"You cannot go now," Dad said.

"Why not? Mom said it was okay!" I told Dad.

"You have to unpack your boxes," Dad said.

"I did!" I said.

"Oh Lena, I forgot to tell you, more arrived today,"

"Okay," I mumbled.

I ran inside, and then I tried not to look at the chandelier. Once I start looking at it, I cannot stop. That thing is crazy big! Then, I dashed into my room. Luckily, I did not get lost! Yippie! I took out a poster and hung it up.

Operation Unpack!

***

I finished in 45 minutes. This room felt more like me now. Except, it still feels a little weird, but I had no time. I felt a vibration in my back pocket. I pulled out my phone to see that Lucy texted me:

Where are you???!!! My Mom made me do my math homework already! 🙄

I am coming! I had a little more unpacking to do, but I will be there soon! 🙄

I replied.

You better be! 😡

Lucy replied 3 seconds later.

I rolled my eyes before I rushed out the door. I stopped to knock on Lilly's door.

"Come in!" Lilly yelled. Lilly was having a tea party for her dolls like she usually does.

"Hi Lilly," I said.

"Oh, it's you," Lilly said, looking up. "Well, we need to talk." I rolled my eyes. Lilly's talks were about strange things. Last time, she thought I made it rain because I was the one who did not want to play hopscotch.

"What now?" I asked her.

"My room is weird, and it's all your fault!" Lilly said.

"Oh really?" I asked.

"Yeah, because you need to go to school," Lilly said. I was about to say something to keep that conversation going, but I knew better. I instead changed the subject.

"Do you know where Mom is?" I asked. Lilly sighed.

"In the kitchen," she said, picking her teapot up.

"Thanks," I said. I zoomed out the door and into the kitchen.

"Mom!" I yelled over the blender. Mom turned the blender off.

"Ready?" Mom asked me.

"Yup," I said, grabbing my backpack. I put on my boots. I said goodbye to Dad, and we left. Two minutes later, we were at a house like ours. Mom knocked on the door. Once, twice. Finally, the door opened. I saw a woman with the same brown hair and blue eyes as Lucy.

"Oh, hello! You are Lena?" she asked.

"Yes," I said.

"Lucy! Lena's here!" She called. Lucy appeared in the doorway with a pencil. She really was doing her homework already.

"Lena!" Lucy said.

"Hello," I said.

"So, come inside," the woman said. Mom and I came inside.

"Emily," Mom said, putting out her hand.

"Amanda," the woman said.

"You two go up to Lucy's room and do your homework," Mom said.

"Oh, Emily, come sit down!" the woman said.

Why am I still calling her "the woman?"

Because I did not know who she was yet, it would not be polite to call her by her first name.

"You better do your homework. No funny business!" Mom said. She did the "I'm watching you" sign while she followed the lady to the living room. I giggled.

"My mom does not like to play around," I told Lucy.

"Neither does mine," Lucy said back.

"Oh, so that was your mom?" I asked her. Lucy nodded.

"Well, if both our moms do not like monkey business, we should get on the move," Lucy said.

"You are right," I said back. We go to Lucy's room. The two of us sat at a desk.

"So, what do you have to do?" Lucy asked, taking out her binder.

"I have to do my electives," I told Lucy.

"Okay," she said, walking to her bookshelf. She came back to her desk and gave me one of the pencils. "Let's get started," Lucy said, sitting down. I got my binder out and got out the paper.

Chapter 4
Fixing Friendship

We were done an hour later.

"So, do you want to see the horses? Lucy asked me as she slipped her binder into her backpack.

"You bet I do!" I said.

"Follow me," Lucy said. I followed Lucy to the end of her room. There were two glass doors. Lucy slid them open.

"Horses!" I exclaimed.

"Yup!" Lucy said. Right there in Lucy's backyard were three horses.

"Wow! Can we go down there?" I asked.

"Of course!" Lucy said.

"Okay, last one there is a rotten egg!" I said, taking off.

"You mean a smelly horse!" Lucy said, taking off behind me.

***

"Wow! They're so beautiful that I don't even care that I'm a smelly horse!" I said as soon as we got outside. Lucy laughed.

"This one is mine!" Lucy said, petting a horse.

"Woah, Woah, Woah!" I said. "You never said anything about owning a horse!" That last part came out more like a squeal.

"My mom rounds horses up, so of course I would have one. Also, this is horse town! Everyone rides!" Lucy said.

"How long have you been riding?" I asked.

"Since I was two," Lucy answered.

"Wow! That has to be some kind of record or something!" I said. "Why are the horses here anyway?" I asked.

"My mom wants to make sure they are healthy, but we can go riding if you want," Lucy said. That second, my face lit up like it did when I got my gift on my 11th birthday.

"Let's do it!" I said.

Fifteen minutes later, Lucy's mom saddled me up onto a horse.

"There you go!" Lucy's mom had said with a grin before she went back inside.

"Um, yah?" I said, flicking the reins softly. The horse started moving. "This is awesome!" I said as the horse went faster and faster, trying to catch up to Curly.

"Lena! Time to go!" I heard from the house.

"I've got to go now."

"Okay, bye!" Lucy said.

"Bye!" I said.

***

The next day at school, I asked Lucy, "Why do you and Mary fight?"

It was 11:30 a.m. in the cafeteria at school during lunchtime, and I was determined to know what happened. Lucy took another bite of her sandwich, chewed slowly, and swallowed hard.

"Well," Lucy said. "Mary never liked me from the start, so I never liked her." She turned her head.

"Don't think for one second I'm going to believe that," I said.

"Fine," Lucy said. She looked at Mary, who was chatting with Riley and looked back at me. Then, Lucy lowered her voice. "We used to be friends, best friends really, but then, one day when I convinced Mary to ride a horse, she fell off. Falling off a horse is no big deal, really, but Mary took it the wrong way. It's been this way for four years."

"Ouch!" I said.

"Well, I don't care anymore," Lucy said.

"Ring! Ring! Ring!" went the bell. It was now time for recess, and I had a plan! I gave Mary my address and told her to come to my house at 10:30 a.m. tomorrow. I told Lucy to do the same, but I didn't let them know that the other was coming. It was going to be my first Saturday in Norco, and I was going to fix their friendship!

***

"Ring! Ring! Ring!" went my ballet dancer alarm. A lot of bells, right? I woke up and fixed up my room. What? Today I was going to see Uncle John, Aunt

Sophie, Grandma, and Cousin Keila for the first time in person since I was nine! I was just making sure my room was clean enough. Grandma was extremely strict when it came to organization. Sometimes, I see her as a more sensible copy of Lilly. Aunt Sophie is more like a copy of me, and Keila is Aunt Sophie, and Grandma combined. Uncle John is like a funnier version of Dad. I just can't wait to see them. Today is going to be the best!

"Knock, knock!" I heard on my door.

"Come in!" I said. Mom came in.

"I scheduled about an hour with your friends in the amusement park," Mom said, walking farther into my room.

"Thanks!" I said.

"So, exactly why do you want to go to the amusement park instead of staying home and helping Dad and Lilly set up some furniture in the attic?"

"What about helping you?" I asked.

"Well, someone has to drive you," Mom said.

"Oh, yeah," I said. "Well, I'm going to fix Lucy and Mary's friendship," I said.

"Well, if anyone can do it, it's you!" Mom said, ruffling my brown hair.

"I'm going to go get ready for breakfast," I told Mom. Then, I went to the bathroom. I used the toilet, took a bath, put on my clothes, and brushed my hair. Then, I went downstairs for breakfast.

"Pancakes!" I exclaimed when I saw my favorite breakfast on the plates.

"Eat quick. Your friends will be here soon!" Mom said. I gobbled a whole pancake into my mouth at once.

"Lena!" Lilly scolded.

"What?" I asked. I meant to say what, but my mouth was full. I know I shouldn't be talking with my mouth full!

"Lena, don't talk with your mouth full," Dad said.

"Fine!" I said after swallowing my food.

"Ding dong!" the doorbell went. My heart skipped a heartbeat. I wasn't so sure about fixing Lucy and Mary's friendship anymore, but I knew I couldn't pretend that no one was home! I went to the door expecting to see Lucy or Mary, but instead, I saw Lucy **and** Mary!

"Oh, no!" I said. Lucy and Mary were outside, in front of my house, and their backs were turned. I gulped and opened the door, but that probably wasn't the best idea because the second I opened the door, Lucy and Mary started fighting.

"How dare you spy on my invite!" Mary yelled at Lucy.

"Did not!" Lucy yelled.

"Did too!" Mary yelled back.

"Did not!"

"Did too!"

"Di-"

"Girls! Calm down!" Lena's mom said.

"Lena, I thought your friends liked each other!" Dad said, wrinkling his eyebrows.

"Well," I said, looking around. Mary and Lucy's backs were turned, they were facing away from each other, and their arms were crossed. I wasn't sure what to do anymore, so I just closed my eyes.

Mom must have noticed because next, she filled Dad in. "Lena said that she is trying to help Mary and Lucy become friends."

"Okay, could you do that outside?" Dad asked.

"Okay!" Mom said, getting up. "Girls! Ladies!" Mom said, clapping her hands. Lucy only moved one eye. Mary did not move at all.

"I think we have a carnival to get to," Mom said, getting her car keys.

"Yeah! Come on!" I said, pulling Lucy and Mary along. I managed to get them out the front door, and they walked by themselves from there. Mary sat at the far right in the back seat, and Lucy sat at the far left. I expected they wanted me to sit in the middle so, I sat in the passenger's seat with a grin. Mary and Lucy looked surprised. Mom started up the car, and the car started to move. I looked back at Lucy and Mary. Lucy was staring at her boots, and Mary was looking out the window.

"So, this is good," I said, trying to get a conversation going.

"What's so good about it?" Mary muttered.

"Here we are!" Mom said, parking next to a white car. I got out of the car.

"Wow!" I said when I spotted a path. This small path led to some tents with games in them and the good stuff, a Ferris wheel, roller coasters! Plus, a bunch more rides I have never seen before.

"I know! They bring it out once a year! There is also the summer fair in the summer, which is my favorite event besides all the Christmas stuff!" Lucy said, bursting with excitement. Well, it was good to see my friends were back to normal; well, one of them anyway. Mary was looking sort of angry.

"Okay, here you go, 20 tokens for each of you, so that means twenty rides. Use them wisely!" Mom said, handing us each some yellowish coins.

"Let's go!" I said, running to the path.

As soon as we got to the amusement park, I could hardly control my excitement.

"Okay, meet you at this bench in half an hour," Mom said, pointing at a bench.

"Okay! You do what you want, and I'll go to -" I looked around. Popcorn! Roller coasters! "This, twisty... thingamajig!" I said, settling on a ride.

"Okay!" Mary said, then headed towards the Ferris wheel. Lucy gulped and followed.

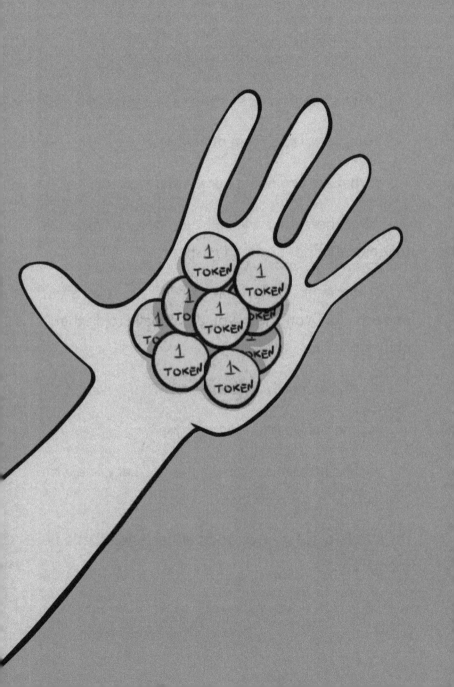

I saw Mary dig her hand into her pocket for tokens.

"What's happening?" I asked myself.

"Ah-ha!" Mary said as soon as she found tokens.

"Um," Lucy said from behind Mary.

"What are you doing here?" Mary asked.

"Well, here, take these," Lucy said, pulling some tokens out of her pocket. I gasped.

"Um, thanks," Mary said, taking the tokens out of her hand. "You know, you didn't have to do that," Mary said.

"Well, I wanted to… because…. ." Lucy said.

"Come on! Do it!" I said to myself.

"… because I miss you as a friend," Lucy said with a smile.

"Well, actually, I do too!" Mary said. "Let's be friends again."

"Deal," Lucy said. Mary and Lucy hugged each other and smiled, and so did I. I mean, "Mission Fix Friendship" had succeeded! Yes!

"Here, take this," Mary said, giving Lucy a letter.

Lucy read it out loud:

"Dear Lucy, you are the best friend I could ask for. Your BFF, Mary," Lucy read. "We are best friends again, but I think we are a group of three now,"

"Yeah, Lena. Ooh! That reminds me," Mary said. Mary whispered something in Lucy's ear. Then they went to the if-you-knock-the-bottles-down-you-win-a-teddy-bear tent.

"Oh well," I still had a ride to get to.

***

I came back to the bench very dizzy. That thing was number one on my list to do next year. It was fun! I rode it 20 times! I spent all my tokens! I saw Mary and Lucy were sitting on the bench already. Oh, and they had a teddy bear! Lucy stood up and grabbed the teddy bear.

"Here, this is for you," Lucy said, handing me the teddy bear.

"To the best friendship fixer ever! From Mary and Lucy," it read on the tag.

"Aw, thanks!" I said. I saw Mom coming back with a bag. As soon as she was here, she placed the bag on the bench.

"Ooh, what's in it?" I asked.

"See for yourselves!" Mom said, grinning. I peeked in the bag. Inside were at least ten bags of delicious buttery popcorn! My favorite!

"Yum!" I said.

"You three can take yours now, and I can drive you over to Lucy's house, okay?" Mom said.

"Hm hmm," I said with a mouth full of popcorn. What can I say? It's **so** good!

"Oh, Lena!" Mom said. We all laughed.

Chapter 5

Getting Back on the Horse

Fifteen minutes later, we were on Lucy's balcony. We were staring at three extremely beautiful horses.

"Can we go down there?" Mary asked, which I thought was weird.

"Only if you want to," Lucy said with a sigh.

"Then, let's saddle up!" Mary said.

"What!" Lucy and I said, startled.

"Ha! You guys should have seen yourselves! You practically jumped!" Mary said, laughing.

"Wait, are you sure you want to go down there?" Lucy asked, walking towards Mary.

"Yeah!" Mary said with a suspicious smile across her face.

"Okay!" Lucy said, taking a deep breath.

***

Twenty minutes later, we were all saddled up! Fine, only Mary. Lucy was almost finished, and I, well, I only had on a helmet. Mary was about to start moving, so I moved out of the way. I sat on Lucy's mom's rocking chair next to the teddy bear Lucy and Mary gave me.

"Okay, yah!" Mary said, squeezing her horse with her legs. Mary's horse ran fast, and the way Mary was controlling the horse was like a professional. It was almost as if she had been practicing!

Lucy got up onto Curly, looked at Mary, looked at me, looked back at Mary, and started speaking.

"Hey Mary, were you practicing behind my back?" Lucy asked as if reading my mind.

"Maybe!" Mary said with a smile as her black ponytail was catching the wind.

"Really? You were?" Lucy asked, picking up her reins.

"Yeah! At the McDole's farm, I use Rosy from the barn!"

"Cool!" Lucy said, about to take off, before I asked, "Where's that?"

"Across from the barn," Lucy answered. "Have you been to the barn yet?" Lucy asked me.

"No, but I think I passed by it on the way to school!" I exclaimed, getting up.

"Okay," Lucy said as soon as I was standing next to her.

"So, it's across from there," Lucy finished.

"Cool," I said, placing my hands on the fence.

"Let's catch up to Mary!" Lucy said, leaning forward into the saddle. Curly started moving, picking up the pace bit by bit.

In about a minute, Lucy was all caught up with Mary.

"Can you do this?" Lucy asked Mary. Then, Lucy took her feet out of the stirrups and on the saddle without any sign of hesitation. Then, Lucy took hold of the reins and straightened her body until she was standing completely on the saddle! Curly did not even slow down for a second the whole time.

"Can't do that yet, but I can do this, though!" Mary said, taking her own feet out of her stirrups. Mary then tossed her legs to one side of the saddle and took hold of that hook on a saddle. I don't know what it's called yet, but I can ask Lucy later. Then, Mary let the rest of her body fall. The only thing keeping her moving with the horse was her hand which was still on the hook.

"Wow, you guys are really good trick riders!" I said with a smile.

"I think I'm going to rename this horse Trickster!" Mary said with a grin. We all laughed. Suddenly, I saw something move in the woods.

"I see a, a… a horse!" I said as the dust cleared.

"Trickster, stop!" Mary said. Because the horse's real name was Quale and not Trickster, he only slowed down a bit, but that was enough for Mary to lower her legs and run to where I was.

"Oh no! The horse is hurt!" Mary said with a gasp, and sure enough, the horse's leg was bleeding. Not much, though; it looked like how my finger did once when I cut my finger with scissors when I was six. My mom didn't want me to use sharp scissors back then, but let's just say I forgot.

"Hurt?" Lucy asked, lowering herself. Lucy pulled on the reins, and Curly came to a complete stop. Trickster (aka Quale) was still running around.

"Yeah, hurt," I said. "Get your mom!" I told Lucy that it if anyone knew what to do, it would be Lucy's mom. Lucy jumped off Curly and dashed into the house. Lucy came back 2 minutes later with her mom.

"There!" I said, pointing into the woods.

"Ooh!" Lucy's mom said, moving closer.

***

An hour later, a big brown horse was sitting, or is it called "laying," in front of me. The horse put its head into my lap, and I started petting him.

"Looks like he likes you!" Lucy's mom said, taking off her gloves.

"Is he okay?" I asked.

"Sure, but it would be sweet if he had something to eat!" Lucy's mom said with a grin.

At that moment, Mary, Lucy and I ran into the house. We found a bowl of apples on Lucy's kitchen counter. We each grabbed a few apples and ran out with them.

"Here you go, fella!" I said as we gave the horse apples. Soon the horse was racing around as fast as I have ever seen a horse go!

"Wow! I'll name you Speedy!" I said. We all giggled.

"Mrs. Brown, can I ride him?" I asked Lucy's mom.

"Hmm? I want to see if he is okay, but I can tell Lucy to text you the answer. If he is okay, you can ride him at eight with Mary and Lucy, and if he still needs a little while for his leg to heal, you can ride another horse from the barn. Lucy can text you with more information. Sound good?" Lucy's mom asked.

"Yeah," I said. "Okay, got to go. See you at eight!" I said, heading for the door.

"Wait!" Mary said. "Friendship hug?" Mary asked. We all smiled and pulled in for a hug.

"We should be called the LMLs!" Lucy suggested.

"That sounds like M&Ms, the candy! Now you're making me hungry!" I said.

"Well, it fits because we are the sweetest girls in town!" Mary said.

"Okay, see you!" I said, running into the house. Mom had already left, I know, because she texted me:

Hi sweetie, I left Lucy's house already.

Be back by lunch.

There's a surprise! 😄

Ever since I read "surprise," my stomach has had the good kind of butterflies in it. As soon as I walked out the door, I only had to pass one house until mine. I recently learned that Mary's house is the white house across from mine. As soon as I walked into my front door, there was a familiar face in front of me. Can you guess who it was?

"Keila!" I cried, throwing my arms around my cousin.

"Lena! Keila said, hugging me tightly. Hopefully, Keila is not as annoying as Lilly. As soon as Keila let go, Uncle John came and picked me up.

"LC!" He said, spinning me around.

"Why, is it not Lena Carls!" Aunt Sophie said, grabbing me from Uncle John and spinning me around some more. I was getting dizzy when she put me down. "Wow! You got heavier since last time!" Aunt Sophie said with a grin.

"Come to my room!" I heard then. I saw Lilly dragging Keila up the stairs. Lilly was not really *dragging* Keila, Keila was walking herself, but Lilly was holding her hand. I was going to follow them, but I needed to say hello to Grandma first, so I walked towards her.

"Hi, Grandma!" I said, hugging her.

"Lena dear!" she said. "Look how much you have grown!" she said, smiling. I smiled back and went upstairs to Lilly's room. I found Lilly and Keila sprawled on the floor, opening Lilly's tea party set.

"Oh, Lena! Will you join us for a tea party?" Keila asked in a sophisticated voice.

"Okay!" I said, sitting at a table. I don't always join Lilly's pretend tea parties, but today seemed like a good day. Lilly and Keila soon brought the tea set to the table.

***

By the time we had had four tea parties, six games of Scrabble, and uncountable games of hide-and-seek (Lilly's idea), it was time to go to Lucy's house, and she texted me:

My mom says Speedy is great! Come to my house, and my mom will drive us to the barn. Cannot wait to see you! 😶

I texted back:

See you there! 😉

I raced into the kitchen to tell Mom.

"It's time to go!" I said.

"Okay, your father will take you!" Mom replied.

"Dad!" I said, walking into the living room.

"Oh! Time to take you, right?" he asked.

"Yup!" I said. Soon, my boots were on, and I was out the door. We were walking. On the way, I told Dad as much as I could, you know, considering how close me and Lucy's houses were. I told Dad about

74

Michael, the horse we found, and Miss Salmon and how she loves to give us more work.

"It's better for your brain; she would always say!" I explained. Dad laughed.

"That's what my teacher said when I was young!" he said.

Even though, throughout this book, adults have been boring and way too normal, they are part of our family, and we still love them anyway!

Dad knocked on Lucy's door, and Lucy answered 5 seconds later.

"Lena!" Lucy exclaimed.

"Hi!" I said. Once we were in the living room, I saw Mary.

"Hi, Mary!" I said.

"Hey!" Mary said, getting up from Lucy's black couch.

"Lena, I will pick you up here in an hour and a half, okay?" Dad said.

"Okay!" I replied.

As soon as Dad left, Lucy's mom came into the room.

"Who's ready to ride the night away?" Lucy's mom asked.

"Me!" Lucy and Mary said. I have to admit, that had been a pretty wonderful day.

We all hopped into Lucy's mom's red car.

"We are here!" Lucy's mom said five minutes later.

"Wow!" I said as I got into the barn, which had seven stalls. The left row was cut short because of a ladder. It led to a hayloft with not too much hay. Each of the stalls had a smiling horse in them. Or at least I think they were smiling. It's kind of hard to tell.

"Hey, Rosy!" Mary said, petting a pretty, white horse.

"Okay!" I replied.

"Hi Curly!" Lucy said. I soon found Speedy's stall.

"Hi again!" I said, opening the door to his stall.

Twenty minutes later, we were all saddled up.

"Promise we'll always be friends forever," I said to Mary and Lucy.

"Promise," they said.

We all raced off into the moonlight together.

Epilogue

That's a pretty remarkable thing that happened to me, right?

Well, don't worry because it's not the end forever. Look for "Lena Carls and The New Additions."

Well, bye for now, friends!

Don't be afraid to tag along on the ride! All you have to do is get:

Lena Carls and The New Additions #2

Glossary

The part of a book where you can find the meaning of some words you might not have understood.

Balcony – A place connected above the ground outside that is protected by bars

Budget – A money plan

Chandelier – A fancy decoration usually hanging at the top of the dining room or hallway

Determined – You really want to do something

Electives – Classes you get to choose to take in some middle school, high school, and college

Grin - A type of smile

Hardly – Very little or not much at all

Honest – Another word for the truth

Impatiently – Waiting in a mad mood

Intermediate – Middle or in between

Jaw – The bottom part of your face/mouth

Muttered – Whispering in a way that is hard to understand.

Obvious – Already clear

Reigns – A strap that you put around a horse's head so that you hold it in your hands to control a horse

Saddle – What you put on a horse that you sit on and keeps you from slipping off

Saddle Up - The act of getting a horse ready

Scholars – Smart people

Sensational – Something wonderful or incredibly good

Sophisticated – Extra fancy or has a way of fashion

Stirrups – What you put your feet on when riding a horse. Stirrups can come in handy when getting onto a horse

Extras!

Turn the page for a word search, map of Lena's house, school, and town! Plus, a sneak peek of Book 2!

Word Search!

Find all the words below in the letters!

Lena Friendship Moving Carls Ride Horses

```
DM CSTFBU.GNMYRWMSAXVUOP FTYAED
ESXAFRDSETGHFEWFHUTLENAFDWGASV
SDERDEASCVI OIMOLPSXAZXEWTFGUIO
CDFLSCVT.YE R UIOPAEDXZWGHESDVSN
WGCSF SRG VF S UFDSGUYDESXAZRTF M
RI DETFEGTH EGH MOVINGTGTEDQCVBH
DFRDCSFTH.Y SBYNFYRDEDGYUI JKOEB
FREINDSHIPHWSTEAFHJDWXETYJKPOR
CVHJKMOVDSWLERATGFSETYUITNAGC
```

Sneak-A-Peek!

Book 2!
Lena Carls and The New Additions!

Introduction

Hi again! Lena Carls here, and in case you are new, I am pleased to meet you! New or not, you have quite some catching up to do, but don't worry. In no time, you'll be up to speed. Now, I have a new baby sister and a puppy! I have met a bunch more people by this time too! I cannot believe I have been in Norco for this long! How time flies, right? Anyway, the story starts now!

Chapter 1
The Big Surprise

"Let's go again!" my best friend Lucy said.

"I forgot about my head for a second!" Mary, my other best friend, said, giggling. We just came back from riding our horses through a brand-new trail that we just found. We ran through a path, and then we were washed out of the trail by a shallow lake. It was really fun.

~ ~ ~

Maps! Enjoy!

Look closely. In each map, Lilly is doing something ridiculous!

Number 1, My room

Number 2, My House

Number 3, My School

See you next time! – Lena Carls, Signing Off

— — —

Author's Note

Hey! My name is Enioluwanimi Solaru. Long! I know, right? That's why you can just call me Eni! I was born in Silver Spring, Maryland, in the United States, and I currently live in Crofton, Maryland, right now! My birthday is May 29. I like to have a party on my birthday! Do you? I have two sisters! Oreoluwa and Temiloluwa (Ore and Temi). I like to read and write in my free time, and I like to write the Lena Carls series because it's my way of talking to kids of all ages! Through stories! I hope you enjoyed the book! Keep reading, and remember, today's readers are tomorrow's leaders!

Reading is like watching TV. And a story you feel involved in, is a great story. I hope you enjoyed this book. Keep reading!

-Enioluwanimi Solaru (You can call me Eni!)

CPSIA information can be obtained
at www.ICGtesting.com
Printed in the USA
LVHW080135251121
704427LV00003B/38